W9-DEE-630

Moving Day

Moving Day

Anthony G. Brandon

Illustrated by Wong Herbert Yee

Green Light Readers
Harcourt, Inc.

Orlando Austin New York San Diego Toronto London

It was moving day.
Mr. and Mrs. Kim were moving.

Jenny Kim was moving.
Jack Kim was moving.

But not Annie.

"I'm not going," said Annie.
She sat on a box.

"Let's go," said Mrs. Kim.
"I'm not going," said Annie.

"You have to go," said Jenny.
"I'm not going," said Annie.

"We all have to go," said Jack.
"Well, I'm not going," said Annie.

"You will have a big yard," said Mrs. Kim.

"I like my little yard better!" said Annie.

"You will have a big room," said Mr. Kim.

"I like my little room better!" said Annie.

"You will make new friends," said Jenny.

"I like my old friends better," said Annie.

It was time to go.

"Annie, get the last box," said Mrs. Kim.
"Okay, but I'm still not going," said Annie.

"Is this puppy going?"

"Yes," they all said.
"Then I'm going, too!" said Annie.

Pack Your Suitcase

Pretend it is your moving day.
What special things will you pack?
Make a suitcase to carry them all!

construction paper

pipe cleaners

magazines

scissors

crayons

glue

hole punch

1 Fold the paper in half.

2 Make a handle for each side.

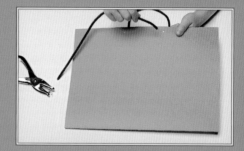

3 Fill your suitcase with pictures.

Ask a friend to guess what is in your suitcase. Then show and tell what you have inside!

Draw Your Dream House

What would your dream house be like? It can be big or small. It can be any color you want it to be. Maybe you would like to live there with your friends or family—or maybe you would like to live there all by yourself. You can build your dream house with your imagination!

markers,
colored pencils,
or crayons

 paper

1. Draw a picture of your dream house.

2. Write about your dream house.
Write why you would like to live there.

3. Share your dream
house with a
friend.

Meet the Illustrator

Wong Herbert Yee likes drawing animals—especially animals wearing clothes! The rabbit in *Moving Day* is special to him because it is his daughter's favorite stuffed animal. He likes to put that rabbit in every story he illustrates.

©1998 Santa Fabio/Black Star

Wong Herbert Yee

Copyright © 2003, 2001 by Harcourt, Inc.

All rights reserved. No part of this publication may be reproduced or transmitted
in any form or by any means, electronic or mechanical, including photocopy,
recording, or any information storage and retrieval system, without permission
in writing from the publisher.

Requests for permission to make copies of any part of the work should be mailed
to the following address: Permissions Department, Harcourt, Inc.,
6277 Sea Harbor Drive, Orlando, Florida 32887-6777.

www.HarcourtBooks.com

First Green Light Readers edition 2005
Green Light Readers is a trademark of Harcourt, Inc., registered in the
United States of America and/or other jurisdictions.

Library of Congress Cataloging-in-Publication Data
Brandon, Anthony G.
Moving day/Anthony G. Brandon; illustrated by Wong Herbert Yee.
p. cm.
"Green Light Readers."
Summary: Annie Kim does not budge when her family tells her it is time to
move to their new house, but then she notices the new puppy with them.
[1. Moving, Household—Fiction. 2. Korean Americans—Fiction. 3. Animals—Infancy—Fiction.]
I. Yee, Wong Herbert, ill. II. Title. III. Series: Green Light reader.
PZ7.B73677Mo 2005
[E]—dc22   2004022692
ISBN 0-15-205646-7
ISBN 0-15-205652-1 (pb)

C E G H F D B
A C E G H F D B (pb)

Ages 5–7
Grade: 1
Guided Reading Level: E–F
Reading Recovery Level: 8–10

Green Light Readers
For the reader who's ready to GO!

"A must-have for any family with a beginning reader."—*Boston Sunday Herald*

"You can't go wrong with adding several copies of these terrific books to your beginning-to-read collection."—*School Library Journal*

"A winner for the beginner."—*Booklist*

Five Tips to Help Your Child Become a Great Reader

1. Get involved. Reading aloud to and with your child is just as important as encouraging your child to read independently.

2. Be curious. Ask questions about what your child is reading.

3. Make reading fun. Allow your child to pick books on subjects that interest her or him.

4. Words are everywhere—not just in books. Practice reading signs, packages, and cereal boxes with your child.

5. Set a good example. Make sure your child sees YOU reading.

Why Green Light Readers Is the Best Series for Your New Reader

- Created exclusively for beginning readers by some of the biggest and brightest names in children's books

- Reinforces the reading skills your child is learning in school

- Encourages children to read—and finish—books by themselves

- Offers extra enrichment through fun, age-appropriate activities unique to each story

- Incorporates characteristics of the Reading Recovery program used by educators

- Developed with Harcourt School Publishers and credentialed educational consultants

Daniel's Mystery Egg
Alma Flor Ada/G. Brian Karas

Moving Day
Anthony G. Brandon/Wong Herbert Yee

Animals on the Go
Jessica Brett/Richard Cowdrey

Marco's Run
Wesley Cartier/Reynold Ruffins

Digger Pig and the Turnip
Caron Lee Cohen/Christopher Denise

Tumbleweed Stew
Susan Stevens Crummel/Janet Stevens

The Chick That Wouldn't Hatch
Claire Daniel/Lisa Campbell Ernst

Splash!
Ariane Dewey/Jose Aruego

Get That Pest!
Erin Douglas/Wong Herbert Yee

My Wild Woolly
Deborah J. Eaton/G. Brian Karas

A Place for Nicholas
Lucy Floyd/David McPhail

Why the Frog Has Big Eyes
Betsy Franco/Joung Un Kim

I Wonder
Tana Hoban

A Bed Full of Cats
Holly Keller

The Fox and the Stork
Gerald McDermott

Try Your Best
Robert McKissack/Joe Cepeda

Lucy's Quiet Book
Angela Shelf Medearis/Lisa Campbell Ernst

Tomás Rivera
Jane Medina/Edward Martinez

Boots for Beth
Alex Moran/Lisa Campbell Ernst

Catch Me If You Can!
Bernard Most

The Very Boastful Kangaroo
Bernard Most

Skimper-Scamper
Jeff Newell/Barbara Hranilovich

Farmers Market
Carmen Parks/Edward Martinez

Shoe Town
Janet Stevens/Susan Stevens Crummel

The Enormous Turnip
Alexei Tolstoy/Scott Goto

Where Do Frogs Come From?
Alex Vern

The Purple Snerd
Rozanne Lanczak Williams/Mary GrandPré

Did You See Chip?
Wong Herbert Yee/Laura Ovresat

Look for more Green Light Readers wherever books are sold!

CECIL COUNTY
PUBLIC LIBRARY
301 Newark Ave.
Elkton, MD 21921

E Fic BRA
Brandon, Anthony G
Moving day